RAVAGED

MATE FOR THE ALIEN MASTER
BOOK 2

L.V. LANE

CONTENTS

CHAPTER
ONE

HARPER

I hear approaching footfall, heavy against the mesh flooring of the spacecraft.

Then his lower legs come into view.

Boots. Really big boots.

My palms become clammy, my breath a shallow pant… and I wonder if he's proportional?

My timing really sucks.

Seeming to know exactly where I am, he crouches and his face also comes into view. I nearly pee myself. It's not that he's ugly, far from it. There is a compelling quality to the symmetry of his humanoid face with those strange curving horns nestled within thick, black hair. He's just freaking huge… and strange, really freaking strange. My mind keeps trying to overlay him with human traits, but the proportions are all wrong. It's like shifting sand, except nothing is shifting; it's all just configured slightly wrong.

He's wearing black futuristic armor that molds to his insanely built body. At least, I presume it's his body and there's not a twig-like being under there.

A thick forearm braces over his thigh, with a great, shovel-sized hand at the end—no, definitely not a twig. As he flexes his fingers, claws spring and retract.

I shudder.

"Tiny, frail human. What are you doing in there?" he rumbles, voice so deep, I feel it vibrate through my chest.

"Hiding?" I say. I sound confused about the fact that I'm hiding. Why do I always sound confused?

"Not hiding very well," he counters. Smirking that slightly too wide, too many teeth smile, he reaches for me with that huge, shovel-sized hand.

Then I wake up…

Like seriously, I wake up. My timing sucks all around. I've had this same dream for months now, on never-ending repeat like my very own groundhog day.

Once again, I'm both frustrated and annoyed by my mental timing. I have a strong suspicion that the fierce alien would do wicked things to me if only he could… grasp.

I sigh. I want to grasp the dream so that the alien might grasp me, but it's fading now. I can't even work out why I want this. More likely, I'd faint than experience a sexual epiphany if he'd gotten a hold of me.

I shouldn't keep mentally referring to him as the alien. His name is Quinn, and I 'met' him in a book by Avery Sinclair.

Does this make it worse?

I think it makes it worse.

The buzz of my alarm reminds me that it's Monday and I need to get ready for work. It's freezing in my bedroom, and I have to force myself to push the covers back and haul my ass out of bed.

My life has gone down the drain. It's little wonder I'm dreaming about hot aliens—also, those books. Avery Sinclair has a lot to answer for. No real man can compare to the aliens in her stories. I need to stop reading the damn books. But it's like a kind of addiction. Every night, I lay in bed and gobble up some more. The bitch needs to stop writing so I can finally get a life.

I'm being unfair. She's not a bitch at all. Well, maybe she is? Given I've never met her, I don't know either way. Maybe she's a man? Men masquerade as women writers sometimes, I heard.

Now, I'm disturbed by the prospect of Avery being a man.

Why does that bother me?

The linoleum flooring (who would even use that in a bedroom?) is like ice under my feet as I pad through to my tiny bathroom. It's the size of a coffin in here. A sink, a toilet, and a shower crammed into enough space for one of those things. I go. Reluctantly, I take my pink nightshirt off and turn the shower on.

It takes me five minutes to get the minute adjustment right on the lever so that I'm not being scalded or frozen. The tiled floor is even colder than the linoleum in the bedroom, and I hop from foot to foot as I fiddle with it. The moment I step under the weak spray, someone uses water in a neighboring apartment and blistering water pelts me.

I snap it to colder. Great! Now I'm freezing!

"Fuck!" I mutter. "I fucking hate this shower! I fucking hate this apartment!"

Shivering furiously, I squirt shampoo into my hand and scrub my hair like a maniac. My feet are going numb, and I can't feel my fingers by the time I finish rinsing off. Today, I'm going for broke, and I risk tapping the lever oh-so-slightly toward hot.

Bliss!

How low has my life sunk that a thirty-second blast of temperate water equates to living the dream?

Not wanting to spoil the moment of perfect water temperature, I finish my shower in record time. I've become adept at it by now. Dragging the shower curtain out of the way, I step out. As per usual, it's like a cold sauna in here. There's a tiny, glazed window that won't open, and the extractor fan is broken. Reporting it a dozen times to the snooty property manager hasn't helped. I guess my asshole landlord will fix it at the same time as he fixes the oven.

I dry, I dress, I grab some toast and a coffee.

I leave my tiny apartment with the peeling walls and double deadlock for another day working at the small convenience store.

Moving to another town wasn't easy, and I'm glad I got a job. My abusive ex wasn't always abusive. For the first year, Ned was a regular mechanic who loved tacos, craft beer, and binging Sci-fi movies on Netflix.

Then a new guy joined the garage crew, and Ned fell into drugs.

The debt he racked up on our joint credit card wasn't the worst consequence.

He's cleaned himself up, again, or so he says. Fool that I am, I believed him the first time he told me this. It was only later, after we had split for the second time, that one of his former girlfriends called me up and said he had done this before.

Bruises: they fade, but the reason they came to be there leaves a permanent scar.

I'm still young. My friends keep encouraging me to embrace life again. But I don't want to date, not yet anyway. Is it wrong to be so jaded?

I just want to escape reality with my books. It's safe in there. Avery Sinclair guarantees a happy ever after. While things can get a little rough, I know it will work out by the end.

I need that guarantee. Because to be blunt, my life so far has failed to deliver one for me.

My day passes as per usual. I'm on the checkout for a while. I do some shelf stacking. I snag a packaged sandwich at lunchtime—one of the perks of the job. I chat to Joel, a teenager with a crush on the girl who works in the bakery next door as I eat my ham and cheese on rye. Then I stack more shelves, and mop the floor out the back after a carton of milk is dropped. Finally, I complete another hour on the checkout before it's time for me to leave.

It's not a bad job. The people I work with are nice.

But I'll be honest, I can't claim to be living my best life.

I'm not living. I'm existing while I lick those mental wounds.

As I near the entrance to my apartment, I notice Ned waiting, leaning against the wall, pulling on a cigarette, and radiating tension.

I tense, too. Seeing Ned has that impact on me. His shiny new pick-up truck is parked a short distance away. He got a loan for it, he said, off a guy he knows. We're not together anymore, but it still makes me feel sick inside to consider the kind of guy he's gotten this loan from. We both had to declare bankruptcy after the credit card debt. It's a year on, and I'm only now building a tiny nest egg again.

I can't do this. Not again. I'm about to turn away when he spots me.

Cold washes over me, followed by an urge to empty my stomach—a thousand emotions crash through me as our eyes meet. The memory of how simple and easy our relationship once was, is bittersweet, and overridden by the roadkill it became.

The memories still have the power to assault me.

The fist marks on the walls.

The tears.

The guilt.

The last dollars taken without permission from my purse because he needed another fix.

Some cracks can't be plastered over. Sometimes you need to take a bulldozer to them, grind all that trauma into dust, and start again somewhere new.

Dragging a breath into my starved lungs, I put one foot in front of the other until I'm standing before my ex.

"How are you doing?" Ned asks.

"Good," I say. My feet are killing me, I'm hungry and tired, but I don't say any of those things. I've tried polite small talk, and it only drags the moment out.

"I'm doing good," he says when I don't ask the question.

Fuck, this is awkward. Why does he keep doing this?

"Ned, I—"

"Babe, fuck, can we just talk?"

Taking a step back, I shake my head. He goes to put his hand on me, and the white-hot panic that consumes me is so sharp I get those dizzy sparkles in front of my eyes.

"Don't!" I say. My voice is sharp and brittle.

His hand falls to his side.

"I won't fucking hurt you."

Again, floats between us.

"Please, Ned. Don't come around. I'm glad you're doing better. But I can't do this."

Shaking, I brush my hot tears away and take the open stairs two at a time all the way to the third floor. I don't want to cry over him, but they spill regardless.

It's not until I'm inside with the double deadlock in place that I can let go. My legs feel like cooked noodles and barely take my weight. I'm going to be sick. Stumbling through to the bathroom, I heave up nothing until I'm a trembling mess of snot and tears.

When I'm done, I wash my face, brush my teeth, and chug a glass of water down.

Not bothering with food, I climb into my cold bed, open the reading app on my cell, and disappear into a book.

CHAPTER
TWO

QUINN

"You reported a stowaway?" I ask the ship's captain as I enter the vessel.

"Yes, sir!" he says. "Our sensors detected an unexpected weight. Oxygen levels suggest an unexplained life form on board. All crew are accounted for."

I nod. My nose picks up a tendril of her scent. Human scent. "I will apprehend the culprit," I say.

My boots ring against the mesh flooring of the spaceship. I've walked this path to the storage room a hundred times, and every one ends the same.

As I hit the lock to open the door, her sweet scent fills my lungs. There, tucked between a row of meti-plastic crates, is the cause of my nightly grief. Blonde hair pulled back into a ponytail, and dark blue eyes, which, although small, appear large in her tiny human face.

Delicious. Human females, as I have recently discovered, smell fucking delicious.

Crouching gives me a better look at her, further emblazoning the image on my mind.

My claws spring and retract. Since these dreams first started, I've come to worry about my claws. Fucking and killing can be confusingly similar to the primitive side of me. I've never touched a human, but I can tell that her body is flimsy compared to mine. She could be shredded should I touch her with my claws and is defenseless before my much greater size and strength, even without.

"Tiny, frail human. What are you doing in there?" I ask.

"Hiding?" she says in a tentative voice like she's confused about whether she is hiding.

Then again... "Not hiding very well."

A strange feeling burrows in the center of my chest every time we meet. The tiny waif appears lost in ways beyond her presence as a stowaway on this ship. Each iteration seems to stamp this determination more deeply. I convince myself her scent is a little stronger, more familiar. The details of her delicate face further enrich. Her hair is not only blonde but a thousand different shades. Her clothing, a pink smock-like covering, has the image of a furry creature on the front and the words, *I love bears, bedtime, and books.*

I want to protect her. It has been many years since I felt urges for anything beyond warring.

I want to collar and leash her and make her into my human pet. Only then will she be safe.

She would make an excellent pet. My fingers itch to skim over the delicate column of her throat as I imagine how it will look when my collar is there.

Then I wake up...

"Fuck!" I mutter, realizing that I've shredded my bedding again. I'm in bed, in my quarters, alone.

Why do I always wake up before I've gotten a hold?

I never dreamt about humans before the one belonging to Haden entered my life. Now I can't stop thinking about the small impractical little beings.

I'm a Ravager. It's in my nature to ravage, whether it's killing an enemy or claiming a mate.

I want to claim her, the little blonde waif who invades my nightly dreams. To bury my cock and hook so deeply she won't walk straight for a week.

Heaving myself out of bed, I clean up and toss on some clothes. I will talk to Avery about this.

The corridors of the fortress are black and imposing. The whole structure is carved out of a sheer mountain face. Given it snows constantly here, it is always fucking cold. Not that it bothers me, I've gotten used to it over the years. But the human seems to feel it for I find Avery entombed in a thick, fur-trimmed crimson coat when I enter the common room. Haden, her life-mate, is present at her side.

The common room is exactly that, a great hub of sorts with tables and chairs in the center, a wall of food replicators on the left, and another area with low seating to the right. A wide, curving window looks out across the snow and ice mountain range that predominates this region.

It is both beautiful and frigid.

Kane sits opposite Haden and Avery. The Devlin male faking civilized as he sips a protein juice. He has become as obsessed with human females as I have. It all started with the arrival of the one Haden claimed as his mate and bonded slave. Not that I covet Avery. She's too wild for my liking and has a filthy fucking mouth. According to Haden, humans come in all different colors. I asked Avery if she could find me a green one as it has long been my favorite color—she rolled her eyes.

Shortly after this, I started having strange dreams. Which was when I discovered that humans do not, in fact, come in green or even blue. The lack of a full color palette seems a bit of a shortfall in their species, but that is not my problem.

The human who invades my dreams, is.

At the replicator I place an order before heading over to the table where Kane, Haden, and Avery sit.

"Did you dream of your human again?" Kane asks conversationally.

I drop my data tablet on the table.

"Yeah," I say. "You?"

He nods and goes back to his protein drink.

Yesterday he slaughtered a Narwan patrol single-handedly. Except for the one he kept alive to watch while he roasted and ate their fallen companions. Well, he didn't eat the whole of them; I believe it was a sample. Then he sent a survivor back with a message, fuck off our claim, carved into its head.

That's what this is about, after all, a claim. Resources are scarce in the universe. Haden's people discovered a particularly lucrative kind of mineral in their lands.

And so, a decade-long battle began between them and the people they share the planet with. The Narwan are a woolly insectoid race with eight legs, high intelligence, low empathy characteristics. They are native to the planet, unlike Haden's people who settled here a millennium ago.

I'm a mercenary. I came for the money and the joy of killing because that's what I am now.

I wasn't always bitter.

Once upon a time, I had a home-world and people I cared for. Then the war came through, and everything was turned to dust. According to Haden, I'm merely a side character in his story.

Well, fuck that. I don't know how she was doing it, but Avery Sinclair, the writer, found a way to control our lives. Not anymore, Haden shut that shit down. Apparently, the computer she used to craft her evil magic has already been destroyed.

So now we are all free. But what does free mean? Has some other being now gained similar godly control?

It makes my head hurt just thinking about it. I consider myself an uncomplicated male with uncomplicated principles. Trying to grapple with the concepts of space time continuum is well beyond my capability.

But all the stuff with the dreams is making my head spin. Somehow, it's all started again, and not only me; Kane is caught up in this too.

"Mine appears to come as a package deal," Kane continues. "But I don't want the second one."

This is a new development.

Avery is staring at Kane. She has forgotten to close her mouth as she eats, and it hangs open in a very unattractive way. Haden leans over and pushes her slack jaw shut before petting the silky-looking hair on her head. Scowling, she picks up her drink.

"A tiny, noisy mini-human," Kane says. "It is always clinging and making demands. I do not want the smaller one. It is not very stable on its feet."

"You never mentioned this before!" Avery says, shooting daggers at Kane.

"I did not think it was important," Kane says with a shrug. "It looks small and deformed. Is there a way to get rid of it?"

Avery, who had chosen this inopportune moment to take a drink, spits it out.

"What? No!" Avery splutters, making like she is about to clamber over the table and assault Kane. She is incredibly feisty for such a small species. Haden calmly snags his mate around the waist. "You are all fucking savages!" Avery rages. "That's a child. No, you cannot get rid of it! Do not dream about the mother again!"

Kane frowns.

"She is mated?" Kane says like a pitched battle is not taking place on the other side of the table as Haden attempts to subdue the wriggling bundle of feral he has placed upon

11

his lap. The replicator dings behind me, but I don't spare it a glance.

"A child? As in offspring? This cannot be right," Kane says, shaking his head slowly. "I have definitely seen the female self-pleasuring using a small pink magic wand. No female would self-pleasure if she had a mate. No wonder the offspring is so small and weak. It would be a blessing to ease its suffering."

"It's a fucking child, you moron!" Avery rants. "No, you can't ease its suffering! What do you even mean by ease its suffering? What the fuck is wrong with you? What the fuck is wrong with everybody here?"

The battle ends when Haden stands, tossing his mate over his shoulder. He stabs a finger at Kane. "Do not mention the fucking earth women again. See what you have done? Now I must punish my mate just to settle her down!"

He stomps toward the door while his mate beats upon his back with her small, weak fists. "This is not a punishment time!" she wails.

"It is always a punishment time," he counters as the door shuts around them.

The occupants of the room go back to eating now that showtime is over.

The replicator dings again, reminding me of my food.

Reminding me, too, that I had questions I needed answering.

"She has anger management issues," Kane says, staring after the closed door. "I wonder if they all do?"

"No idea," I say. Grabbing my broiled ratkin out of the replicator, I bite off the head and crunch it between my teeth before taking a seat at the table with Kane. "I'm a warrior. I've spent more time thinking about being with a human than is healthy," I say, waving the ratkin body in Kane's general direction.

He waves a hand like I was offering the food to him. Scowling, I take another bite.

"Me too," he says. "Given I cannot kill the small, deformed human that clings to mine, which Avery has indicated is offspring, I'll have no choice but to take them both."

"You plan to claim her then?"

The books, which Avery wrote in her past life on earth, have opened a gateway between her former world and ours.

As I chew on the last part of my ratkin, I reflect that the laws of creation have been sabotaged by Haden's dark-haired mate. My dreams are solidifying, becoming sharper with every iteration.

Will I finally touch my female in the way that Haden came to touch his mate?

I don't have an answer.

I do have duties, and they occupy my day until my night can once more belong to her.

CHAPTER
THREE

HARPER

"Just another day in paradise," I mutter to myself as I bite into my tuna on rye. Joel isn't around today. He finally built up the courage to speak to the girl in the bakery next door. They're eating lunch together in the local park.

The kitchen-come-breakroom of the convenience store where I work is a cupboard-sized space with a small, cracked table and two worn faux leather chairs. I suspect the chairs have been here since the seventies; the mud green color is not so popular anymore.

Spread out before me is my notepad, pen, and cell, which, although tiny and at least five models out of date, is good enough to search for apartments and jobs. I have an aunt in south Florida, so I think I will avoid there. This time I'm not leaving a forwarding address with anyone but my parents, so I'm not expecting Ned to follow me. But either way, I want a clean break, and I'm thinking about another state.

My parents moved to Canada two years ago for my dad's job. He's on a working visa. I could move in with them for a short while. But I'm a grown woman, and I feel defeated thinking about tucking my tail and fleeing back to them.

Also, they have my younger brother with them, and he is going through a rebellious stage. They have enough to deal with without me turning up at their door.

I sigh as I thumb through the apartment listings. You don't get much for your money anywhere, so I will need to line up a job promptly. I want to do this, and I want to stand on my own two feet. Now that I've resigned myself to moving again, I feel motivated. I moved here in a rush and didn't think through the availability of work. I didn't think about much of anything at the time.

This time, I'd like to plan properly. Maybe somewhere with a good local college where I can take some vocational training. It will get me out where I can hopefully meet some real people.

Yes, I recognize my obsession with a certain alien is not healthy. I've spent too long hiding from life—time to change.

Finishing my sandwich, I toss the wrapper into the trashcan. I have a few possibilities jotted down, and I'll do some more research tonight.

A sudden commotion comes from beyond the closed breakroom door. My head swings around, and my heart rate picks up in the way of a person too recently attuned to danger. I want to go and see what is happening.

I also want to hide or run.

My chair scrapes across the tiled flooring as I push it back. I have yet to determine what I'm going to do but standing in readiness makes me feel better.

The giant crash is startling; my heart feels like it's lodged in my throat. I need to open the door. I need to stop cowering in this breakroom. My fingers fumble with my cell as I hear raised voices. Maybe I'm oversensitive after all the crap Ned put me through. Yet there is a tone to trauma, and whatever is unfolding in the convenience store ticks all the boxes.

"Harper!"

Ice floods my veins. That voice and that roar; I have heard it's like too many times.

Ned.

My lips tremble, and my hands shake. What the fuck is wrong with him? Why does he do this? Just why?

It wasn't only Ned I left when I left my home town, it was my friends. I speak to Tammy most weeks. *"Girlfriend, you need to file a restraining order, or he's never going to stop,"* she said when we spoke over the weekend.

Fuck! Why do I keep hoping that this is all going to magically stop? It's not going to stop. He's here, in the small convenience store that doesn't deserve to be decimated because he can't handle his failings.

Taking a deep breath, I yank the door open. I need to deal with this.

Outside I find the rack that holds deodorants and toiletries has been tipped over, and the contents are scattered across the floor. The shop owner is waving a hand, telling Ned to calm down. He has his cell in his other hand. I don't know if he's called the police yet or is about to, but either way, none of this is good.

"Ned! What the fuck are you doing?" My voice is brittle. I'm shaking, and my heart is racing so fast I can hear it pounding in my ears.

"Babe, I just want to talk to you."

I shake my head.

"No," I say. "You don't get to do this. You don't get to invade my life." I consider myself a pacifist; I don't have a violent bone in my body. But the blood is pounding through me so fast and so fierce, I'm gripped by a terrible desire to slap him across the face. It's only the sure knowledge that slapping him would escalate the situation further that keeps my hands at my side.

I hate him, I realize. I've experienced so many emotions

since this all began two years ago. I pitied him; I pitied myself. I've been frightened, angry, betrayed, and hurt on a thousand levels. Somehow the memory of how it had once been between us overshadowed all the terrible events enough that I didn't hate Ned.

But today, in this tiny convenience store, I hate him with every fiber of my being. I hate him in a way I did not think myself capable of hating anyone.

As he lurches forward, the stench of alcohol wafts over me. I step back, both hands out. "Don't!"

"Harper! Are you okay?"

My stomach knots hearing Joel's voice.

A red haze settles over Ned before he swings around. Since we separated, he's become convinced I'm sleeping with someone, not that it's any of his business.

The store owner is on his cell talking to someone—I'm presuming it's the police. None of that is happening quickly enough, and when Joel, the sweet gangly teenager who doesn't have more than fluff on his chin, throws himself between Ned and me, it's a red flag to my ex.

Ned punches Joel. Ned's a big guy used to heavy work. Joel is nothing but long limbs and bones.

I scream.

Joel drops. I've never seen a person drop like that before. It's like someone cutting the strings on a puppet, and he slips gracelessly to the floor. I lean over his prone body. "Get out!" I scream at Ned. "Get the fuck out!"

His arm swings, and I cower, expecting a blow. But all he does is rake through a nearby shelf sending tins of baby formula crashing to the floor. Turning, he flees.

"Joel!" I turn back to the poor young man who is far too chivalrous for his own good. The girl from the bakery rushes in and throws herself down to the other side. Joel's eyes flutter open, and I heave a deep, relieved breath in.

The wail of sirens follows. Finally, now that Ned has gone, the cops arrive.

Joel groans and hoists himself to a sitting position. The owner checks on Joel before hastening to meet the arriving police.

I can't move. My legs won't follow my command. I'm still kneeling on the floor I was due to mop before leaving tonight. Head in hands, I burst into tears.

The rest follows in a blur. The police take statements. Someone, I think it might be the girl from the bakery, sits me in one of the mud-green faux leather chairs and gives me a cup of tea. Beyond the tiny breakroom, I hear someone clearing up the shop.

I should go and help, this is my fault, after all, but my legs still don't feel steady.

I'm given a number I can call tomorrow to get the ball rolling on a restraining order.

I'll be honest, I'm a little numb through most of this.

I can't believe Ned came here. I can't believe he trashed the shop where I work.

Somewhere along the line, I've forgotten what it is to feel safe.

I'm staring blankly at my half-drunk tea when the shop owner comes into the breakroom. The chair makes a screeching noise as he pulls it across the floor and sits opposite me.

"I'm so sorry," I say.

He returns a watery smile.

There's a plain white envelope in his hand. He sets it on the cracked surface of the table and pushes it toward me.

"I wish I could give you more, Harper," he says as I fix on the envelope with a blooming sense of dread. "But I've got my own problems to deal with, and I can't have violent exes turning up and destroying my shop. My mother-in-law had to go in for hip surgery, and she doesn't have insurance. My wife's stressing about meeting the hospital payments as it is, and this place doesn't turn much of a profit. I'll give you a good reference. You're a hard worker. I've no complaints, you know that. But everybody knows everybody in Redwood. Word will get out, and then folks will stop coming to my shop."

I nod. "I understand," I say. Only I don't understand, not really. I want to tell him how unfair this is. I want to toss the stupid envelope back at him and tell him to keep the money. But I don't because I still need to pay my rent and eat. This isn't his fault, and it's not fair on him either, and I get that he has his own problems.

But fuck it, I wasn't ready to move yet.

"The police said they will take you home," he says. "They've not been able to find Ned yet."

Picking the envelope up, I force myself to stand. Now it's over, I just want to go home and wash this bad feeling off. I don't think Ned will be waiting at my home, but I wasn't expecting him to come here and do this either, so what do I know?

I go home. The police officer checks my apartment and reminds me to call the number tomorrow.

I undress. I take a shower that's miraculously at the right temperature.

Then I crawl into bed, open my reading app on my cell, and try to forget about all the problems I'm going to have to deal with tomorrow.

CHAPTER
FOUR

QUINN

"We have a breach in sector two," Layton says as I enter the briefing room.

"I've not even sat down yet." I point out.

The green-skinned bastard gives me a withering look. Layton is Haden's operational assistant, and he manages all the work allocation… and other stuff that is way beyond my paygrade. I'm a mercenary, I understand my role here is to do and not think, but sometimes it grates.

I applied for residency a few weeks ago. I'm not alone in deciding to settle here. There's plenty of conflict, so I'm not often bored. Boredom is as good as a death sentence to my kind. We need to keep our claws sharp, so to speak, or mental rot can set in.

Not that there are many of my kind since my home-world was decimated.

"There is a breach in sector two," Layton repeats. He is a slight male and no more than half my height. Lamandas come in various green shades, but Layton is particularly iridescent in the morning sunlight that streams through the window.

His big, black eyes blink a few times before he smiles. "I could allocate Kane to the breach if you prefer?"

"Fine, don't burden me with the details," I mutter. About facing, I stomp out of the briefing room. The bastard knows how to bait me. It's been over a week since we had a decent breach, and my claws itch in anticipation of a showdown.

The whole mountain on which the great city of Xars is built is riddled with mining excavations. I'm surprised the thing hasn't collapsed. It keeps the structural engineers busy for sure.

That's not my problem; security is.

There are four-hundred and fifty-two mining sectors. At any given point, five percent are out of commission due to a breach.

As I hit the elevator bank where the twenty mesh cages drop into the great yawning chasm, the engineering crews are piling out in a chaotic melee. Some even have a bit of green blood showing, which is unusual. At the first sign of trouble, the sector should shut. Barriers drop, allowing the engineers to evacuate. Then one of the allocated security guards goes in and kills all the raiders.

I prefer the mine breaches to the skirmishes topside. Knee-deep snow just slows me down.

The elevator rattles as it takes me down—the temperature drops as I descend. There is yet more screaming emerging from below. Rolling my shoulders, I prepare myself to battle the Narwan band pillaging sector two.

At the bottom, the lift cage rattles to a stop. It's fucking freezing the lower you go. Yet more screaming, green-skinned engineers emerge from the corridor for sector two at a run.

I frown.

This is not normal.

My ear communicator beeps, and Layton's smooth voice assaults my right ear. "The barrier has failed. Narwan have reached the engineering hub. I'm sending backup."

"Fuck," I mutter, taking off along the corridor at a run. I'm the only one passing in this direction as yet more engineers flee.

At the end of the main entry tunnel, it splits off into a network of smaller tunnels. The Narwan drop shafts from above ground in the hope of hitting a mine. Given the mountain is nothing but tunnels, they hit pay dirt often. Mostly, they reap whatever minerals they can and run. The southern slopes of the mountain are warm and temperate. But the northern peaks, where the rich minerals are found, are cold and inhospitable to all but the Narwan who are native to the region. Snowstorms are constant, making it near impossible to locate raiding parties.

Although the Narwan are not the only problem we have on Xars.

My nose tells me which corridor to take. There are no more screaming Lamandas engineers. There is only me and whatever the fuck is waiting at the breech.

A Narwan sentry is waiting at the next junction. I see its multifaceted single bug-eye widen as I slide underneath its legs and open its belly up with my claws.

Blood sprays and it emits a high-pitched screech—their death noises are particularly unpleasant on the ear. Bringing my controlled slide to a stop, I barrel into the next one, knocking it onto its back.

A dozen Narwan are scuttling over the supply cache where the big-assed mining bot lays dead and smoking after its disablement with an explosive charge.

Dropping the cache, the Narwan converge on me as one.

My horns rotate into attack position as I double extend my claws. Issuing a battle cry, I lower my head and charge. I rake, slash, and skewer. Their blood sprays to the chorus of high decibel screeching. Here, right here, is where I feel alive. The Narwan are far from defenseless, and I feel the sting of pincers and take a beating from their many legs. But I'm a highly weaponized life-form, powerful and deadly for any who stand in my way.

They fall, one after another, until the corridor and former mining bot are covered in lumps of wool-covered flesh and sprayed with blood.

Breathing heavily, I survey the scene. Dead. All are dead... except I spin to find not a Narwan, but Kane leaning casually against the wall. The Devlin's tail swishes from side to side. The fucker is smirking.

"Layton thought you might require assistance," he says. "But it looks like you've got it covered. Also—" He indicates the lumps of steaming flesh. "You have cut them into convenient meal-sized portions for me. So that saves a bit of time."

I roll my eyes. A wasted gesture since I'm covered in blood, and Kane likely can't see it.

At the distinctive sound of scuttling legs from the corridor behind him, Kane leans up from the wall. His tail lashes out, stabbing the Narwan dead center of its big bug-eye.

I admit, I'm impressed.

The Narwan screeches as Kane's razor-tipped tail jerks back out. The Narwan does this weird backflip and thrashes about in noisy death throes.

I wince. As much as I enjoy killing Narwan, the noise is grating.

Kane turns back to me. "I have discovered something about the wormhole Haden used to collect his small, verbally offensive mate."

My claws retract, and my horns rotate back into neutral, curving down past my ears. "Go on," I say.

The fucker grins. He knows he's got me. But I see the same instincts clamoring in him.

The arrival of the cleanup bots breaks the impasse.

"I suggest you take a shower and join me in the common room. I can't hold a conversation with you while you smell like food."

CHAPTER
FIVE

HARPER

Today has been difficult.

The police finally caught up with Ned and had a chat with him. The store owner has decided not to press charges, so there is nothing more they can do. I guess he didn't want the extra stress.

I've been told the restraining order won't be as easy to do. The court is unlikely to approve one without evidence to back it up. Since I never pressed charges at the time when he was being an asshole, there is no evidence to provide.

I feel stupid and naive on a thousand levels for not dealing with this before. Yet how can I blame myself? Who imagines a scenario where their ex turns up and trashes the place where they work?

I'm sure I'm not the first victim of abuse who presumed the best. We humans come with an innate sense of trust until someone takes it away.

Now, more than ever, I know I need to leave.

I still have the boxes from when I moved here tucked at the back of a cupboard, and make good headway on packing my meager possessions. In between filling boxes, I continue my planning. Once more, I'm forced to move in a rush. At least my early research has provided me with a few half-decent options. Settling on a city, I have six apartments lined up to review when I arrive next week. I even have a couple of job interviews for Monday the following week.

Yes, next week.

My dream life feels more tangible than this great upheaval that will see me move to another state. Lucky my asshole landlord has waived the full notice period. Thank goodness, because my small nest egg is not going to stretch very far.

It's been a long day, and I'm rummaging in the cupboard for something quick and easy to eat when there is a knock on my door.

I freeze. My heart becomes a hammer in my chest, and for a split second, my mind completely blanks out.

"Harper? It's me, Tammy! I brought takeout, babe."

My thudding heart slows, and my legs go weak as relief crashes through me. I told Tammy I was leaving, but I wasn't expecting her to turn up at my door. It's a two-hour drive for her, and she works long hours at the hospital where she's a nurse.

The double deadlocks are unlocked, and I open the door.

It's not only takeout since there is a bottle of wine in her other hand.

I smile.

"Babe!" She throws an arm around my neck and plants a kiss on my cheek. "Jason is picking me up later. He's catching up with his brother."

It feels good to have company. I can't remember when I last did something as simple as eating takeout with a friend. We spread the takeout cartons out on the dining table, pour the wine, and set the world to rights.

"I wish you didn't have to go," she says. We're both stuffed and have pushed the plates aside. "I could act as a

26

witness. I've seen the bruises—I've seen how he was with you."

"It takes more than that," I say.

She nods, face turning downcast. "Yeah, I know. It just pisses me off that Ned can do this, and you're the one who must leave. And it's like another state. I can't turn up with takeout and a bottle of wine."

I know what she's saying. The chance of us catching up again in person like this is going to be small. She has a busy job with shift hours. I'll be far enough away that most people would fly.

"I feel weirdly good about the move," I say. "My mom called earlier, asked me to come and stay with them while I figure out what to do next. But it feels like defeat, you know?" My mom had all but booked a flight for me, although I know they can't really afford it. I think it helped me to be stronger, knowing there's a little safety net waiting for me. "And I always wanted to see Colorado."

"What?" Tammy sits bolt upright. "That's like freaking thousands of miles away!"

I shrug. "I know. I want a clean break. I'm not telling anyone the address besides my parents. I'll keep the cell number, but I won't accept calls from any numbers I don't know."

She sighs. "You could stay with your mom and dad. It's not wrong to want to give yourself some space before you rush into a move. You don't have a lot of stuff. I could stash it in my spare room while you're working things out."

"Thanks, Tammy," I say. "I was so worried about everything yesterday. But today, I feel like I'm finally on the right path."

She tops off my glass before lifting hers to mine.

"To new beginnings, babe," she says as our glasses chink together.

"To new beginnings," I agree.

I'm buzzing a little by the time Tammy leaves. We're also a little teary when Jason picks her up.

In the silence that follows, I slide the double deadlocks into place and put the empty cartons in the trash. I stack up the plates and glasses, and for once, leave them until morning.

After sorting out stuff all day, I'm tired, but I know the moment I turn out the lights, my mind will start going over everything, and I won't get to sleep.

As I slip inside the bed, I pull up my reading app, determined to have half an hour of a book to occupy my busy mind. It's the series about the mining planet, Xars, where Quinn lives and battles the Narwan. I'm near the end of the third book. I might even finish it tonight. As soon as I start reading, I tumble into the world. It's like I am there with them, battling the giant spiders as they attack the mines.

My hands get cold outside the covers holding my cell, so I swap them over often.

"Oh?" I say as I read *The End.*

I frown. I scroll back and forward a few times to make absolutely sure. She has a lot to answer for, Avery Sinclair, the writer. I have wasted much of my real life living in her worlds.

Time I should have spent... doing what I don't fucking know.

I'm feeling disgruntled that she left it on a cliffhanger. As I lay in bed, my cell cast aside, the reading app still open, I question my life and the direction it has gone. I'm still young. I can still turn this around.

But the wounds go deep. I'm about to move again, this time to another state.

I wish it were another planet.

Wouldn't that be nice?

Well, maybe not Xars with its constant snow and ice.

I wonder when the next book is out? Maybe it's already out. It didn't mention another book, but no one got a happy ever after, which is not Avery's usual style.

Picking up my cell again, I search for the next book.

Nothing. Not even a preorder.

Now, I feel disgruntled that she hasn't written the next book.

Why hasn't she written the next book?

Is she dead?

I'd pictured Avery Sinclair as the same age as me, but now I'm wondering if she is a crusty old lady who has croaked it before getting the last book out.

I snigger to myself. No, I'm certain Avery isn't old. But I'm curious about her in a way I've never been before.

I google Avery Sinclair.

Missing?

That can't be right? It's not exactly a high-risk occupation. Writers don't suddenly disappear. But there it is, an article about the author mysteriously disappearing. A half-eaten packet of cookies and a cold cup of tea were found at her home a week after she canceled plans with a friend.

Her ex-partner has come forward and claimed Avery was unstable and had lost touch with reality.

Asshole! I roll my eyes.

As I read down, it states she had started on the fourth Xars Wars book a few months earlier, with a planned release later in the year.

A cold, clammy feeling skitters down my spine.

I don't think Avery is unstable. That doesn't even make a bit of sense. I think she is gone, like really gone.

What about the unfinished book? What about my guaranteed happy ever after?

It's gone, like Avery.

Tossing the cell aside, I frown at the peeling ceiling of my bedroom. There's a stain in one corner where a water pipe burst in the apartment above a few months ago.

Gone.

I'll never get to find out what happens next.

The emotions that assault me are unmistakably the ones of grief. They are the same feelings I suffered when I packed my bag and walked out of the home I once shared with Ned. A single suitcase and a couple of cardboard boxes. That was the sum I took with me after two years together.

After all that has happened, how silly to be grieving for a book? Yet, I invested myself in the world and the characters until they became a part of me.

They are gone now. Lost forever. Stuck in limbo without their happy ever after, just like me.

I sigh. For so long, I have grieved in the real world. Denial, anger, despair, guilt, relief, and burgeoning hope have warred with one another and with me. Avery cannot be gone. She cannot leave me with an unfinished story.

Disappointed and saddened by events beyond my control, I determine that I'm worthy of a happy ending for my life story. But as I close my eyes, it is not the real world that I'm thinking about. It is the world and people I met inside a book.

I want Quinn so badly. The fierce alien warrior has suffered so much in the books by Avery Sinclair, missing author and cruel weaver of words.

I want Quinn more than I want my next breath.

I want to be the reason that he hopes once again.

I want to fall into his world.

I want it with every fiber of my being.

What is real, and what is imagination? Is the world where I work and eat ham and cheese on rye any more important than the one I visit when I sleep? Maybe my dreams are the real world, and this cruddy apartment with the linoleum flooring and broken extractor fan is merely a recurring nightmare?

Maybe if I want that other world badly enough, I can find that alternate universe where Quinn lives and wars.

Hearing approaching footsteps, heavy against the metallic mesh floor of the spacecraft, my heart rate picks up. The room where I have hidden is a storage area. A small amber light in the center of the ceiling provides the only illumination. It doesn't matter how many times I do this, the adrenaline spike and compulsion to hide are just as strong.

I squeeze between two giant plastic crates, trying not to breathe, which is hard when my heart is hammering in my chest.

Then his booted feet come into view. Boots. Those humongous freaking boots.

There is no hesitation in his approach like he knows exactly where I am.

I blink, becoming a little dizzy as I try to stifle my breath.

Then I frown. He hasn't crouched. He usually crouches by now?

Tiny hairs on the back of my neck spring to attention—this is different. I wanted different so badly, but now that it *is* different, I'm freaking the fuck out.

Finally, just as I reach mental melt-down. He crouches.

My chest heaves as his face lowers into view. Compelling. Everything about his too angular, too perfect purple humanoid face is compelling. Today, his strangeness does not seem so strange. Today, he feels familiar.

A thick forearm braces over his thigh, with a great, shovel-sized hand at the end. His fingers make a fist and then slowly relax. No claws spring from the tip.

He smirks. He has never smirked prior to speaking. "Tiny, frail human. What are you doing in there?" he rumbles. His voice is so deep I feel it vibrate through my chest.

"Hiding?" I say, sounding confused. Yeah, I'm still confused about this part.

"Not hiding very well," he counters. Grin growing impossibly wide and shark-like, he reaches for me with that huge, shovel-sized hand.

I don't wake up…

I DON'T freaking wake up! And that huge, meaty hand closes over my upper arm.

"Got you!" he rumbles.

CHAPTER
SIX

QUINN

S he punches me in the throat. "Uff!"

"Ow!" she wails. "What the fuck are you made of?! Are you a robot or something? This is not how this is supposed to go!"

I grasp her small, fragile hand before she can strike me again. "Did you hurt yourself?" I ask.

"What? No!" she says, trying unsuccessfully to break free.

"Good," I say decisively. "You are mine now, tiny human." Standing, I toss her small body over my shoulder and stride from the storage room.

She wails and thrashes about as I stalk the flexing metal corridor toward the exit of the ship.

"I have apprehended the criminal," I say as I march past the ship guards.

This is the furthest I have ever gotten in the dream, and I'm not taking any chances. When I lay down to sleep, I anticipated another frustrating night.

It does not feel like those other times we met… and I have never touched her before.

Now I can think of nothing besides claiming the human female whose scent invades my nose.

As I leave the spaceport and enter the fortress proper, I'm assaulted by a notion of skewed reality. The black stone walls and floors glisten a little brighter than they usually do. The air feels a little cooler, and my breath creates a cloud before my face.

Instinctively, I understand that this is not my universe. This is an alternative universe, somewhere I do not belong. Yet I am here; she is here. We are both here.

Her scent, delicious, feminine human scent fills my nose. Behind my armored pants, I feel my cock lengthen and thicken as I anticipate the rutting that will follow.

"Where are we going?" she cries as she jiggles about on my shoulder.

"Foolish human," I say. "Were you confused about what would happen next?"

I hear her murmur, maybe a groan. She knows. The scent of female lust is not lost on me. I don't know anything about compatibility, but I am determined to claim her in the way all claims are made.

As the door to my assigned quarters looms before me, a sense of urgency grips me. I hit the release on the door and pass through, enclosing us in privacy. *Relief.* Without cere-mony, I drop the wriggling bundle of woman onto my bed.

I swallow.

Leaning up on her elbows, she pushes her hair from her face. The mechanism she used to hold her hair back has broken, and it spills all around her like a golden cloud.

As I come down over her, she fights. Not that it matters to me, I'm a male claiming his mate. I will not be satisfied until my hook is buried and she is screaming my name as she comes. Our great size difference suggests it will be a struggle. But I am determined. That Haden claimed Avery tells me my chosen one will endure. It's true, I am bigger than Haden in every way, and different in that way. I tell myself I can go slowly, but deep down, I understand that I cannot.

I am a Ravager; I am ever faithful to my nature but particularly when fighting or fucking.

When my claws spring, her mouth pops open on a gasp. I grin. She smells of both fear and arousal, and it's driving me fucking wild. "Don't move," I say. "I will be careful."

Pretty green eyes wide, she nods. I believe she appreciates the care I take. My claws are sharp and lethal. They slice through her pink, smock-like covering, sending the tatters falling around her. She lays panting. Exposed as she is to my enrapt gaze, the realization of her tiny form becomes more apparent.

Plump breasts tipped with rose-colored peaks, a slim waist, and a flare at her hips. There between her thighs is the treasure of her femininity.

The place where my cock and hook will go.

It's only now that I wonder about my sucker. I have never attached my sucker, for I have never sought to claim and breed a mate.

My nostrils flare. She emits a small squeak, and I realize that my claws have punctured the skin of her upper arms where I'm grasping. I retract my claws immediately, her distress calming my ardor some. Blood pools, although it is only a small nick.

Leaning down, I lap at the wound, groaning as the taste of her blood explodes across my tongue. My grumble deepens as I pin the squirming woman still and lap all the spilled blood. There are healing agents in my saliva, a throwback to our more primitive days, and she quietens as it goes to work.

"Oh! Please!"

She is squirming again, and I pause, realizing all the blood is gone. Then my eyes lower to her breasts.

When I can tear my gaze away, I find her staring at me, chest heaving and eyes hooded and a little glazed. The healing agents in my saliva can have a potent effect on some lifeforms. She is much smaller than me. Perhaps her body is overwhelmed?

Perhaps she is overwhelmed?

My gaze lowers again. The nipples at the peak of her pretty round tits have grown stiff. Like they are aroused. Watching her reaction, I enclose one stiff peak between my finger and thumb and gently squeeze. Her mouth pops open and she emits a small moan.

I squeeze harder, rolling the tight little nub, watching her face contort and flush. Fuck! I'm so fucking hard watching her reaction. I am ready to pop my hook, and I'm not even inside her yet. I keep testing, pinching rougher and harder until she finally squeals.

"Oh! Please! That's—no! Oh, it's too rough."

"I beg to differ," I say. Capturing her wrists, I pin her hands to the bed where she cannot interfere and continue to torment her pretty nipple. The scent of her arousal is thick and heavy in the air. She likes what I'm doing.

I think she is afraid to show her pleasure for reasons that elude me.

Perhaps she is not convinced I'm a worthy mate?

My gaze is torn between the rapture engulfing her flushed face and the fat nipple swollen and taut with arousal. It is the most natural thing to lower my head and lick.

"Oh!"

I smirk and lick again. My tongue is long and agile, and I wrap it around the stiff peak and tug.

She tries to buck me off.

I think she likes that very much.

Her struggles only bring out my urge to dominate. Her flushed, aroused state further drives me to suck the hardened nipple and half her tit into my mouth.

"Mnnn! Ah, please!"

Her hips are rocking and grinding against me. I believe

she wishes to mate. I suck harder, lashing the peak with my tongue at the same time, enrapt by how engorged it has become.

She has two sides, I remember...

If anything, her reaction is twice as strong when I show my care to the other side. I alternate between both, fascinated by how her body responds when I arouse first one side and then the other. It seems to drive her particularly wild if I suck one side while I pluck the other with my fingers and thumb. I wish I had more hands because there are yet more places I want to touch.

My cock is so painfully hard, trapped as it is behind my armor, that it finally drags my attention from ravishing her pretty tits.

When I lift my head, I see that both plump mounds are swollen and flushed with faint bruising where I have sucked too hard. The peaks are stiff and crimson; the lightest brush of my thumb pad makes my captive human groan and hiss.

But my cock is a source of acute pain, and I need to get my armor off.

"Don't move," I caution, holding her eyes to make sure she understands.

She nods.

I still watch her as I stand. The door is locked. She will not be leaving until she is claimed, maybe not even then.

Maintaining eye contact, I peel away my armor.

She watches me the whole time. Breath ragged, she stares at what I expose in a way that tells me she likes it. Until I let my armored pants drop to the floor when she emits a small squeal and tries to scramble up.

"Steady yourself, tiny human," I say. "I will prepare you thoroughly before I try to mate."

This does not calm her; if anything, it makes her thrashing worse. Growling, my claws spring, my right hand slams into the bed beside her face.

She stills, finally. Eyes wide with fear and chest panting.

"There," I say, drawing a single tip gently down her cheek. "That's better. When you struggle, it brings out my bestial side, and I cannot keep my claws in. If you lay very still for me, it will be easier for me to control it." My hand lowers to shackle her throat. She is so fragile beneath me. I could break or maim her with alarming ease.

This thought helps me to find control, and my claws retract.

"Good pet," I say, watching her soften under the praise. "I'm going to inspect your pussy now. Lie very still for me. It will be difficult for me to keep my claws retracted, but it will make that harder if you resist."

Her throat works under my palm as she swallows before nodding.

It takes willpower to move down her body again, for her tits look like they need further attention, but her pussy is calling me. Kneeling at the bottom of the bed, I spread her thighs.

Her little folds are wet and slick as I gently part them so I might inspect between. I don't see a place for my sucker to go, but her pussy glistens invitingly with evidence of her arousal. Above are more folds. I wonder if the place for my sucker is inside here?

I run my fingertip along the slit fighting the urge to spring my claws. This is not the place for them, but the age-old instinct where claws are used to subdue our own females before we can mate is riding me hard.

When I reach the upper, inner folds, she moans and nearly levitates off the bed.

"Oh!"

I grin. "Are you hiding your pleasure nubbin, human?" I ask. Gathering a little of the glistening juice, I pass my fingertip back and forth over the sensitive spot. Some creatures can hold their genitals inside, and I'm confident the tiny human is trying to resist my advances until she is certain I am a worthy mate.

"I—what?"

More whimpering follows. She bites her lip to try and stifle the sounds, but that only makes me work harder. She is testing me. Trying to smother her response to ensure I'm worthy. "Does it need stimulation, tiny human? Do you need me to coax your little pleasure nubbin out?" Gathering more of the juices, I hold her hip to keep her still and rub the little spot roughly.

"Mnnnn! Ah!"

I'm rewarded with a gasped groan, whimpers, and little mumbled begging.

She likes this very much. I work the spot mercilessly. My cock is spitting lubrication, although I do not think it is needed with a human, given she is now gushing pussy juice.

"Naughty human," I say when the little bud emerges. I was right; she was hiding. The thought of my sucker latching onto this nearly has me coming over the fucking floor. I have never latched before. The sucker is incredibly sensitive, and I cannot imagine the intense pleasure as I milk this tiny nub and encourage her pussy to draw my seed.

As her groaning and thrashing turns wild, the need to taste becomes undeniable.

Lowering my head, I lick.

Then growl. The human is absolutely delicious, and I'm ravenous for more of her offering. I run my tongue all around her leaking pussy before thrusting inside.

Her back arches, and her small, blunt fingers claw at the bedding.

Fucking delicious. I'm much enamored with her breathy gasps and writhing. My long, agile tongue better explores all the folds and treasures of her blooming nubbin, making her knuckles turn white as she grasps the bedding harder.

My dick spits out a blob of lubricant, and my sucker

begins to swell. The writhing human female is near insensible with her pleasure as her slippery juices pour. Our females are naturally dry, and the male must provide the lubrication to enable the coupling. But this filthy little being is absolutely drenched.

Her nubbin is growing. It's very slippery, but I curl my tongue around it and tug-rub in a gentle rhythm that matches that of my sucker.

My tiny pet suddenly goes utterly rigid before nonsense pours from her lips and she humps her pussy against my face.

CHAPTER
SEVEN

HARPER

I wake up panting, my body bathed in sweat, and my heart thudding wildly in my chest.

What the fuck just happened?

I groan, feeling the aftershocks of that insane climax. I've never done that before. Never climaxed from a dream. How is that even possible? I mean, I understand that people do it. I have a vague notion that it's linked to puberty. But yeah, I'm well past that now, and I don't remember it ever happening for me at the time. As I stretch, I feel the slipperiness between my thighs—my nipples are still engorged and sensitive. I've never come that hard when I'm awake. I can't wrap my head around how it happened without being touched and while asleep.

It's Quinn, I realize. That fictional alien can turn me into a ball of female goo just by looking at me.

God help me that tongue of his. Avery did not write that detail into the book. Then there is my nubbin, as he calls it. Human men can't find a woman's clit, so it stands to reason that an alien male would be doubly confused. I wanted to giggle when he used the word. But damn, the feeling of his long alien tongue slipping over it was enough to make my toes curl and eyes cross.

"He doesn't exist," I say, like my voicing of this might douse some reality into my declining mental state. Maybe I'm suffering from a weird kind of stress after Ned trashed my workplace, forcing me to move?

Fuck it, everything about that dream and Quinn was so impossibly real.

Outside my ill-fitting curtains, it's getting light.

As I come down from the high, I acknowledge my headache and that I'm also thirsty.

"Just another day in paradise," I mutter as I heave myself out of bed. I go, I shower, and I brush my teeth. I dress in some comfortable leggings and a T-shirt and tie my hair up in a messy bun. I make some coffee and a slice of toast, munching on it as I check my to-do list on my notepad.

More packing, *check*.

Done with breakfast, I drop my plate and cup in the sink.

The trash can is at capacity after the take-out. I also have plastic bags full of stuff I was throwing out. Better sort that first. Keys in my back pocket, I have loaded up with trash boxes and bags when I hear my cell buzzing against the table. The ID comes up as the shop owner. No, I'm not about to put all this down for whatever he has to say—probably another apology for letting me go, *asshole*.

What if he's had a change of heart?

No, it doesn't matter now anyway. I've already decided. I've given notice on this apartment, and I have new ones lined up. The wheels are in motion. I'm not about to stop.

I exit the apartment, pulling the door shut behind me with my foot.

"I should have taken two trips," I mutter as I navigate the stairs. I can't see where I'm going, and I'm going to break my neck. I vaguely remember something about three points of contact.

Somehow I get all the way down without a mishap. The door leading out back to where the trash dumpsters are found weighs a ton. I put my back to it, brace my legs and heave the heavy-assed thing open. It's got spring loading on it. I've lived here a year, and I know it has a spring loading, and yet the nuances of applying enough force to open the door, yet not so much that I go flying, are ever lost on me.

I'm about as successful at opening the back door as I am at adjusting the temperature on my shower.

Which is to say, I'm not successful at all.

It opens with a whoosh, and all my carefully stacked boxes and bags explode across the ground.

"Fuck it!"

A gust of wind chooses this moment, and food-slimed papers and bags tumble and scatter everywhere.

I sigh.

I go through the motions of chasing my trash to the far corners of the rear parking lot and putting it into the trash dumpster, all the while muttering to myself. I'm lost in the process such that I don't notice the truck. And when I do, I realize that I'm far away from the back door.

I freeze.

Why? Just why is Ned here?

As he pulls the truck up between me and the door, a familiar sickly surge washes over me. I want to run for the door, but my mind is whirling with scenarios. If I run, it might provoke him. The back door weighs a ton. The chance of me opening it and getting all the way up the stairs to my apartment seems slight.

Then again, running feels weirdly overreacting. It's mid-morning. I'm right next to the apartment. Maybe he simply wants to talk and apologize?

I don't run. But I need to acknowledge how low our

former relationship has gone because my instinct is still to run.

The faint creak of the door followed by the thud as it shuts grates my frayed nerves.

"Hey," Ned says. Shoving his hands in his back pockets. "I called by the store. They said you don't work there anymore?"

He manages to make it sound like an accusation, like I should have consulted him. I guess that was what the call was about. I wonder if the owner has called the police. Probably not. Now that Ned knows I don't work there anymore, the owner has no reason to worry.

I don't offer a comment. A few feet separate us, and I'm relieved he doesn't try to close the gap.

"He said you were leaving town?"

I see the tic thumping in his jaw, and it stretches my mental barrier thin.

The words that might diffuse this situation elude me. My lip trembles. Why did I come out here? Why did I chase trash around the damn parking lot like a maniac? Why wasn't I more alert? I don't even have my cell with me.

"Are you fucking leaving town?" he roars when I don't answer his question.

I know running is a bad idea at this point, but my nerves won't take another second in his presence.

I run.

I don't get very far when I feel his arm snake around my waist, hoisting me from the ground.

My scream is cut off when he closes his hand over my mouth. I thrash and fight, kick and rake anywhere I can with my nails. The bastard lets me wear myself out.

I start hyperventilating. I can't get enough air through my nose, and Ned's hand is still over my mouth. The passage of air sounds hoarse and unnatural. It's been a year since I had a panic attack, but I recognize on a distant level what this brain fogging, tunnel vision is all about.

"That was really fucking stupid," Ned says.

I'm so fucked.

CHAPTER
EIGHT

QUINN

I wake up with a roar, for I'm in bed and alone.

"Fuck!"

The buzz of pleasure holds my body captive. Her scent still clings to my skin. I'm sure I'd been holding her tightly enough that she couldn't possibly have escaped.

And yet she has.

I don't even know what her name is, and she has slipped through my fingers again. Now that I've had a taste, there is no going back.

Sitting up, I scramble to gather my wits. My conversation with Kane returns to me too late.

I needed something belonging to the tiny human who is forever hiding on the ship. I search the bed for the elusive strand of hair, which according to Kane, Haden used to search for his mate.

Nothing. There is not a single fucking hair.

The center of my chest aches like there is something fucking wrong. Fear. Why do I suffer fear? I face the Narwan daily, and those grim insectoid fuckers don't even get a rise.

Then there are the barbarian hordes who settled beyond the walls of Xars. Given the Native commission has forbidden the use of weapons, leaving us no choice but to hack through them with only claws or other primitive weapons, they are usually good for a mild adrenaline rush on the occasions when they breach the walls.

But fear, real, gut-churning fear? Even when my home-world was decimated a decade ago, it was never fear—rage, grief, desolation, but never fear.

Where does this fear come from?

Light prickling takes hold under my skin. Our bodies secret many chemicals through saliva and sexual play that facilitate the bonding process. Instinctively, I know this fear I feel is not mine but that of the tiny, weak human I carried from the docked ship.

Rising, I pace, head gripped between my hands. I cannot stand her fear. It is like minute Narwans crawling under my skin. I need to find her, now more than ever. And I need to find her now.

Dressing swiftly, I stalk for the common room where I hope to find Avery or Haden.

Avery is in her usual place, eating something she calls toast. It looks dry and tasteless. I have seen more exciting animal feed. Haden lifts his head at my rapid approach. He sees the look on my face, and he knows what I'm about. Rising from his chair, he thrusts the little human behind him.

"Calm the fuck down!" Haden says.

Kane, who is sipping on a protein juice, raises a brow as I halt at the table.

"I need to find her," I say. I don't mention the fear, but it has risen to a roar in the short time since I left my room and arrived here in the common room.

Avery peeps around Haden. "Did you dream about her again?"

"Do not fucking humor him," Haden growls. "He is unstable."

"You have no room to talk about unstable," I point out. Haden turned into a maniac over his small dark-haired mate before Layton worked out how to stabilize the wormhole. At the time, none of us knew what his madness was about.

My eyes lower to Avery. "What have you been writing?"

"Nothing!"

Her squeaked voice sounds fucking guilty to me. I'm not alone in noticing this; Haden also gives his mate a stern look.

"Did you collect a sample?" Kane says in that irritating as fuck, overly calm voice of his.

My head swings his way. "I did not get a fucking sample. Not that it matters because she is writing again!"

Is the fear my tiny human experiences by Avery Sinclair's design? I stab a finger in Avery's general direction. This is bold and foolhardy on my part, for Haden is her bonded master and does not take kindly to it.

He growls, body coiling like he is preparing to launch himself at me.

Kane springs from his chair like he is also thinking about wading in.

"Don't!" Avery thrusts her smaller body between her mate and me.

Haden growls, grasping Avery's arm and trying to thrust her behind him again.

"Wait! I had a dream!" she says.

We all collectively stop, staring at the human writer who has caused no end of grief in my life.

In all our lives.

My eyes narrow suspiciously. "What sort of fucking dream?"

"I saw you carry her off the ship." Her face turns a deep shade of pink. "And then Haden woke me up!"

"What happened after you carried her off the ship?" Kane turns to me with fake causal interest.

I ignore the nosy bastard. But I realize we are all standing glaring at each other and drawing the attention of the crowded room. Dragging a chair out noisily, I plant my ass on it. After a brief pause, the others follow suit except for Avery whom Haden places on his lap.

"It wasn't a dream anymore," I say. "I touched her." I don't add that I pleasured her, although I am sure it is what they're all thinking. I also don't mention the bonding part, which has led me to storm in here.

"This is not the best place for this discussion," Haden says.

"I need to find her," I repeat. The fear is getting mixed up with other emotions and threatening to spring my claws.

"The wormhole uses quantum physics," Haden says. "It is not best known for its stability, nor for predictable outcomes. As likely you could end up dead as with the human. I still don't understand how both Avery and I came back. But I believe it was to do with the book that Avery wrote while I was in her world."

"She could write another book," I reason. I cannot believe I'm suggesting this. But the fear is laced with bone-deep terror, and one way or another, I need to find her.

"She is not writing another fucking book," Haden says. "We had enough trouble with the last one. Even supervised, her writing is dangerous. Who knows what the fuck will happen next?"

"I'm right here," Avery says.

"I'm aware of your current position," Haden says. "It's no more than an hour since you were punished, but that sounded a lot like attitude. And attitude requires further punishment."

I'm confident every time Haden mentions punishing his

bonded life-mate, he is talking about fucking. "We don't have time for this."

"Fine," Haden says. "If you do not have her hair, we at least know the planet now. We will try and cross-reference her name with a description and have Layton look her up on the intergalactic database."

"I don't know her name," I say, scowling. "It did not come up during the conversation." Our words were brief, and most of them filthy… before I lost her.

"So, you just fucked her," Avery says bluntly. She gestures toward me. "Look at him. They cannot possibly be compatible. You're all fucking savages! I'm not helping him to bring her here!"

Haden closes his hand over the front of her throat, bringing her tirade to a squeaked stop. "Silence, mate," he says. "You have already earned yourself yet another punishment. Any more, and you will not get out of bed for a week."

Her throat bobs under his massive hand as she swallows, and her eyes as they lock upon Haden's are very round.

"I believe that was a poor threat," Kane says, smirking.

"We are compatible," I say, finding myself once more the object of everyone's attention. I don't actually know if we are compatible, but I'm determined that we will be.

"You do not have her name," Kane says. "You also do not have her hair. You do not appear to have anything that might help us to locate her."

"I could go to earth," I say.

"There are billions of people on earth," Avery points out smugly. "You will never find—ummm!" Her words turn mumbled as Haden thrusts three thick fingers into her mouth.

I admit I have only ever considered thrusting my cock into such a location, but the move is surprisingly effective for silencing her… and hot.

"You couldn't help yourself, could you?" Haden says to

Avery, eyes narrowed in a way that does not bode well for her future. Rising from the seat, he sets his mate on her feet, closing a big hand over her nape and giving a little warning shake before turning his attention to me. "Get her name. Get something of hers we can feed into the database. We cannot help you otherwise." With those parting words, he escorts his mate from the room.

"Blood would be best," Kane says, reaching for his protein drink.

"How the fuck am I going to get her blood?" I ask. But then I remember how I nicked her skin when my claw sprang.

Blood. Sweet, delicious blood that I lapped up from her arm. If even a tiny amount is perpetuated in the reality of my room, I will find it, and find her.

CHAPTER
NINE

QUINN

I have spent too many minutes listening to Layton lecture me on the dangers of quantum travel and wormholes.

"I get that," I say. "Now load me the fuck up or whatever you do when opening a wormhole."

Layton sighs and clasps his slender green hands together. His long black robe is impeccable, and his green skin glows in the bright morning sun. "You have not listened to a word I've said," he admonishes, giant dark eyes narrowing upon me.

"I listened to every fucking word," I say, barely holding it together. Harper Reed, is her name, and in my very soul I know she is mine. "I don't know how the fuck it happened, but a bond has been made between us. She is off the fucking charts frightened, and if I don't get to her in the next thirty seconds, you won't like the rampage I go on."

Layton raises a brow. Not much fazes the green-skinned bastard after years working for Haden, so I guess I'm going to have to up the threats. I'm a fucking Ravager, my horns have already shifted to attack position, and my claws keep twitching with the need to spring.

"Fine," he says, unruffled by the prospect of my imminent meltdown. I must admit, the Lamandas has nerves of fucking steel given I could shred his shiny green body in less time than it takes to draw a breath.

He walks with that strangely sinuous gait over to the console and taps away.

It's only now that I begin to wonder about a few things... like how the fuck do I get back?

Too late.

Blackness descends. My eyes feel like they are being boiled in their sockets, and my skin flailed from my body.

I scream, but I hear nothing as my cry is sucked into a void empty of space and time.

Weightless, I twist and turn, mouth still open on the silent cry. There is a strange notion of movement like I'm plummeting from an impossible height.

Light leaks into the darkness as a great spinning orb approaches. Or perhaps I approach it, for the tiny orb grows and grows.

I am going to crash into it.

I am going to fucking die!

I land, knees bracing, the thud of impact so heavy that the gray surface cracks and crumbles under my boots and sends up a shower of dust and grit.

Straightening, I shake off the dust. Her scent hits me. Human female, *my* human female, and fear.

My claws double spring. My horns are already locked for the attack.

"What the actual fuck?"

A male, he also scents of fear.

Turning, I center myself on the voice. I can barely see my little stowaway, lost under the greater bulk of a human male. There is blood on her chin and a red blush on her cheek and jaw. In her wide, terror-filled eyes, I see the manifestation of the fear that pummeled me from across the expanse of time and space.

Mine!

The sight of this male's hands upon her is like a wild fever igniting my blood. I want him off of her, but I don't want to harm her in the process.

She. Is. Mine.

The male suddenly makes a low grunt and staggers away. My nostrils flare, a roar erupts from my chest. My feet are moving with slow, deliberate steps as his face swings toward me.

He steps back, mouth gaping and arms flapping.

I charge.

He sprints toward a shiny metallic ground-vehicle. Fumbling, he throws open the door before slamming it again with him inside. I leap, booted feet landing center of the hood. The vehicle creaks ominously and buckles under my great weight.

My grin is all teeth as I eyeball the human male who dared to harm what is mine. I slam my clawed right hand into the roof... and peel.

There is a satisfying sound of screeching metal. I will peel the whole fucking thing open and decorate the insides with his blood.

A great rumble comes from under my feet.

The fucker is seeking to escape.

My boot slams onto the glass front screen. Thousands of tiny cracks form—another good kick, and it breaks free from the top right corner.

"Quinn!"

My head swings at the sound of my tiny stowaway calling my name. How does Harper know my name?

"Quinn, get down!"

The ground vehicle lurches backward with a screech of

tires. I jump from the hood, landing upon the ground. The vehicle comes to an abrupt stop, and the engine revs.

"Quinn! Get out of the way!"

Then the vehicle surges toward me.

Foolish male, thinking he can win this.

I grin. Letting it come closer until he thinks he has got me, then I roll to the side, double claws raking through tires and metal shredding it in a satisfying way.

The once glistening surface is a tangle of ruined metal. I will do much worse to the male inside if he dares to take another pass.

He doesn't. The engine makes a weak rattling sound as he directs it away and flees.

"Quinn!"

Harper's broken cry captures my attention once more.

Pivoting, I stalk toward my poor, damaged pet.

Tears are streaming down her face. "Oh! What were you thinking?" she wails, small hands feverish as she inspects me for imaginary damage.

"Hush, tiny human pet," I say.

As my hand cups her face, she sobs and throws herself at me.

Mine!

CHAPTER
TEN

HARPER

I understood Quinn's claws were both sharp and lethal, but the power to rake through a truck body is astounding. I might have better enjoyed the sight of him gouging into the metalwork of Ned's shiny new pickup. But I was busy being terrified that Quinn was about to get run over by my enraged ex.

Then he kicked the windshield in. It was like front row seats at the movies where you're afraid to look because you sense it's about to get messy.

I didn't even have time to grapple with the impossibility of Quinn actually being here.

But now trashed pickups, crazy ex-partners, and the exploration of fictional characters coming to life is of little consequence. Cradled within Quinn's arms I finally feel safe.

I blink and sway before giant hands close over my upper arms. We are in my apartment and there is a vague notion that he carried me up here.

"Quinn?" I croak.

His answer is a growl, low, rattling, and full of menace.

57

"How do you know my name?" he demands, aggression rolling off him in waves. If Ned hadn't gotten away, I fully believe Quinn would have killed him.

"I—" I'm going to sound like a nut if I say I read it in a book. But yeah, I did read it in a book. I glance around at the familiar walls of my bedroom… And bed. I swallow hard. I'm in my bedroom and Quinn is here with me.

"Tiny stowaway human, you will answer my question, or I will put you over my knee and discipline you until you do."

He's not bluffing. And damn. That sets off a mini explosion deep in my womb. I think I might have climaxed a little. "That was—um—not a very good threat," I say before I can help myself.

"Do not fucking tempt me," he growls.

"Fine, I read it in a book," I say, feeling his claws slowly flexing and biting into my upper arms.

"Avery Sinclair," he says. "That small human with a propensity for cursing has much to answer for."

I'm about to ask him how he knows Avery Sinclair when his eyes darken and I'm tossed onto the bed. "Uf!" I splutter, pushing hair from my face.

Seeing his claws fully spring, my mouth pops open on a gasp. Humongous freaking claws that could give Wolverine a run for his money. Claws that have just decimated my ex's shiny new truck.

"This is not the time for discussing the nefarious human. Who was the male putting his hands upon you?" he says, crowding me on the bed, and caging my smaller body with his. The bed creaks ominously; I'm not sure the manufacturer had hulking aliens in mind.

This moment has a certain déjà vu. Only last time, I was a stowaway on a ship, and it wasn't quite real. This time he has just tried to kill my ex-boyfriend… And is radiating pissed.

"Who! Was! It!" Inhuman face inches from mine, his claw-tipped fingers collar my throat tight enough to pierce the flesh.

I freeze.

"My ex."

"Ex? What is an ex? A mate?"

"No. Not a mate. He used to be, I guess, although we don't use that word. We used to be together. He's struggling with the adjustment of us not being a couple anymore. Some people are like that. I mean, I don't understand why. They just seem to get super possessive. Like you were with them once, and now they think they own you forever."

I bring my rambling to a stop. His claws retract, and he squeezes my throat in a way that commandeers all my attention.

"You were with me once," he says, tone low and deadly. "This time, you will not escape me. This time I will claim you in the way that all claims are made. After, there will be no confusion about who you belong to. No one will dare to harm you again. If I see a male with his hands upon you, rest assured, I will kill him."

My heart is pounding wildly. This is nothing like the other time. This time Quinn is burning with a fiery, possessive rage.

The hand upon my throat eases away. Quinn's expression is stony. There are no apologies for anything he just said. Lethal claws, recently used to wreak destruction, slice through my clothing. I lay perfectly still; I can feel a sting where he pricked the skin of my throat. I wanted Quinn so badly, but somehow that dream-time experience lured me into false expectations of what and who he is.

There is no mistaking now. Quinn is raw and primal. He is taking and claiming me as a mate, and I am not getting a choice. I should hate his high-handedness. I should be appalled by his primitive determination of ownership over me.

I try to understand the complex emotions that are raging through me as he shreds my clothing away. Quinn is nothing like Ned. There is danger here in the arms of an alien warrior who courts death and violence every day. Yet, there is also protection and an unearthly dedication.

My clothing is reduced to tatters, leaving me naked upon the bed. Here I find myself the object of his intense gaze.

A gaze which has settled upon the apex of my thighs.

I've spent way too long wondering if he's proportional. That dream I had, the one where I climaxed so hard I saw stars, is coming back to me. I recall all too vividly what he's packing behind his futuristic armor.

His nostrils flare. I emit a small squeak as he comes over me again. His gaze has now settled on my heaving breasts and I know he's going to taste. I wriggle. I can't help myself. This is too much, too intense, and he hasn't even started yet. He pins me, a huge hand collaring my throat as his eyes lift to lock with mine.

I'm so overwhelmed.

Never taking his eyes from mine, he captures my right nipple between his finger and thumb and squeezes hard. There is no build-up. He squeezes, pinches, and pets it way too roughly, and my body goes up in flames.

I moan, strain, arch my back and squeeze my thighs together to try and ease the building ache.

His expression turns hooded, and he watches, cataloging my every tormented twitch and cry. My hands, which had fisted around the bedding, grasp his giant wrist and try to pull him off. "Oh! Please! That's—no! Oh, it's too rough."

"My tiny stowaway is lying," he says. Capturing my wrists, he pins them to the bed above my head and continues to torment me.

"Mnnn!" I don't even try to find coherent words anymore. I think there is a danger I might climax from nothing but this touch.

Then he lowers his head and licks.

"Oh!" My memory of his long, agile, alien tongue is not an exaggeration conjured from some depraved corner of my mind. He wraps it around the stiff peak and tugs. Then he sucks deeply at the same time as he lashes it with his tongue, and it feels like the top of my head has just come off.

"Mnnn! Ah, please!"

He squeezes my breasts together and proceeds to drive me wild. I lay panting, trying to work out where the hell I am and what the hell is happening. This time it is a thousand times more intense. This time it is so much more *real*.

Expression dark, Quinn rises, and begins to strip from his black futuristic armor.

My eyes play ping-pong. I want to look. I also don't want to look. But I can't freaking help myself. My breathing turns ragged. I think about running, although where I might go is a mystery to me.

His pants drop to the floor, and he fists that giant freaking cock.

Oh. My. God.

Turning over, I try to scramble up the bed, a squeal of terror bubbling from my throat.

A big hand encloses my ankle, yanking me back down.

"Steady yourself, tiny human," he says. "I will prepare you thoroughly before I try to mate."

This does not calm me, if anything, it urges me to ramp up my struggle. I remember all too well how he prepared me last time.

A low growl is all the warning I get before his claws slam into the bed beside my face.

I'm flipped back over so that I'm facing him again.

"Good pet," he says, smirk showing too many teeth. "Lay very still for me, stowaway. That way, I can maintain control of my claws."

There is no searching for my clit this time. He runs a single thick finger up the length of my pussy before catching the little nub and sending a shockwave through my body.

He grins. "I know where your little nubbin hides, pet," he says, circling it with maddening slowness.

Then he lowers his head and devours me.

"Mnnnn! Ah!"

The sensation of his long, dexterous tongue flicking over my pussy sets me rocketing. He knows exactly how to torture my clit in the best kind of way. Licking it, flicking it, and them rolling his tongue over it until I am a writhing mass of rapturous sensation and climbing high.

"Fucking delicious," he rumbles against my pussy before sucking hard over the little nub.

My breath stutters. I struggle because it's way too intense. Quinn takes my hips in his hands, holds me still, and rips the climax from me.

In the aftermath, I lay panting. Forcing my eyes open, I find him staring at me with a brooding expression.

My eyes lower almost under automation. Between my parted legs, chin glistening with the evidence of my arousal, is a great hulking alien with Herculean shoulders, arms thicker than my thighs, and chest and abs that look like they've been carved from purple granite. Across his chest is dappling in a darker shade. Everything about him is other-worldly hot.

My throat stings where his claws have nicked me. I don't have a chance to worry about that because he prizes my legs further, lowers his head again, and feasts once more.

There was a moment when I thought he might be gentle with me.

He is not gentle. He is too rough and too determined, and no amount of tugging on his thick, black hair will dislodge him from his food.

What is he doing with that tongue? I'm pinned roughly to the bed, my clit so swollen and sensitive that I can barely see straight. His tongue pulls-rubs relentlessly on my clit. I can't decide if I want him to keep going or stop. I have already climaxed, but the wild screams that pour from my lips only drive him on.

I fear I might die if he doesn't stop.

He doesn't stop, and I don't die. I'm stuck in this twisted limbo while he wrings never-ending pleasure from me.

"Please, fuck me already."

Did I say that? No, I can't have done something so stupid.

Lifting his head, he studies me. My pussy is so oversensitive that it throbs like he's still plucking it with his tongue. "You are my pet," he says.

I try to process what he said. I can't.

"Do you need me to pleasure your nubbin further before you accept your rightful place?" My pussy clenches. His eyes narrow in his strange purple face and his nostrils flare. He licks his lips, long tongue passing in a way that makes me shudder. Did he really just have that in my pussy? The gleam in his eyes tells me he's about to do it again, for as long as he needs to, until, in his words, I accept my rightful place.

"Please! No!" My hands wave over my pussy like I'm trying to ward off this huge male. I cannot bear any touch upon my throbbing clit. I might lose my mind if he snakes that alien tongue around it again.

"Agree you are my pet," he demands. "Beg your master to rut your filthy weeping pussy. Beg me to hook you deeply and fill you with my seed. Beg me to latch onto your little nubbin."

I have no idea what half these things are or mean. They sound alarming and hot all at once. And I'm not getting a choice. Either I beg Quinn to further ruin my body, or he will attack my throbbing clit with his tongue. I can't bring myself to look at my pussy, but my clit feels twice the normal size. I'm confident I'm going to freak out if I see what he has done to it.

Then I remember his humongous cock. Neither option is good.

Theoretically, there should be plenty of space in there. I mean, women have babies, right?

I start hyperventilating.

His head lowers while I'm having a mental breakdown, and he spears me with his huge, alien tongue.

"Mnnn! Oh!"

This is nice; wildly nice. He does some kind of twirling thing that makes my eyes cross and my knees shake.

I'm about to come again. I sense it's going to blow all the previous ones out of the water and into deep space.

He stops, and his long, agile tongue flicks all around my clit.

I'm lost. I want to come. I want to come more than I care that his cock is the size of my arm and has weird wriggling tentacles at the top. Maybe I imagined them? Maybe it was a trick of the light?

"Please, I need to come." Vision blurred, I stare down at Quinn, the male who I first learned about between the pages of Avery Sinclair's book. Only he's no longer a character in a book. He is here with me, in this weird alternate reality.

I am at his mercy. If his taunting of my engorged clit is any indication, he doesn't have any.

He spears me again, and all the sensations twist up. Heat bathes my body. I'm so freaking close to detonating when he stops once again.

Panting, I open my eyes to find him smirking. I'm maddened by my need, ready to take matters into my own hands. "Is my little pet testing me?" he asks, gathering my wrists together in one giant, shovel-sized fist like he knows what I'm thinking about. "Be assured, I can do this for many hours and days. One of us will break long before then. It will not be me."

I believe him, absolutely.

Head lowering, he laps all around my pussy, carefully avoiding the places that might deliver the glorious high.

I can't stand it. This is torture. I convince myself his cock plundering my pussy will not be such a challenge.

"Please, make me your pet!" Barely cognizant, I don't care how ridiculous this sounds. I need to come more than I need my next breath. My skin is on fire. I fear I might spontaneously combust with this monstrous strain.

"Tell me to hook your pussy," he demands, lifting his head.

What the hell is a hook? Is he talking about the tentacle things? While I'm still trying to force the words out, he slips one giant finger into my sopping pussy.

I go ramrod stiff. The claw is retracted, but heaven help me if he springs it while he's inside me.

His expression turns calculating. "Stay very still, tiny human," he warns. "I would not want to damage this pussy."

He's taunting me, I reason, but fear and arousal go to war as he pumps slowly in and out.

"That's good," he says. "Just lay there, my filthy little human pet, and let your master have his way." My pussy starts to make wet squelchy noises that bring a hot flush to my cheeks. "Tight and absolutely drenched. I can see you will need to be thoroughly rutted often to keep you satisfied."

"God, please just fuck me," I groan. "Please make me your filthy pet. Please, I need it." Madness is pouring from my lips. I have never been this wet in my life. I've never been this desperate in my life.

Tears spill over my cheeks, and I blink in confusion when he stops.

And something the size of a battering ram tries to spear my pussy.

"Mnnnnn!" I try to wriggle away, but he's having none of it. Face a picture of determination, he pins me to the bed and bludgeons his way inside. I'm so slippery. He is slippery too.

It doesn't matter how my muscles scream in protest, his cock plunges deeper and deeper. With my hips in his hands, he saws shallowly in and out.

"So fucking tight, my naughty little pet," he growls. Hands shifting to my waist, he takes a firmer grip and surges all the way in.

CHAPTER
ELEVEN

QUINN

Deep into my rut, my body takes over. She screams and thrashes as I fuck my fat cock in and out, but I cannot possibly stop. I need to plant my seed in her womb. I need to hook this sweet pussy so deeply it will ruin her for every other male.

The mere thought of other males drives my need to claim and imprint even deeper.

I am a Ravager, and I am assuaging my lust on my filthy little pet.

My cock leaks copiously in a way it has never done before. Our combined juices splatter over the bedding with every rough thrust.

It feels sublime as her wet, gripping pussy welcomes my cock.

It looks obscene as the tiny human is stretched around my fat dick.

We are compatible—just.

Already I know I'm addicted.

She is taking nearly all of me, but I need to get my hooks

into the opening of her womb. Only then will I be able to latch my sucker to her little nubbin and deliver my seed deep. My thrusts slow, taking on a heavy slap that rams my hook against the entrance to her womb.

"Fuck! Please! It's too deep."

It is not too deep. It is nowhere near deep enough.

But my sweet, naughty little pet is suffering from my brutal rutting. Leaning down, I take her throat in hand and lower my lips over hers.

She moans as my tongue spears into her mouth in tandem with my thrusting cock. Soon she is sucking on my tongue greedily for my saliva contains secretions that drive her lust higher and ease her pain. My cock aches in a sweet way as I rise higher than I have ever before. The sensation of my hooks briefly penetrating the entrance to her womb every time I bottom out is a divine form of torment.

She sucks greedily upon my tongue. I have to pinch her face to get her to stop. The secretion will lift her arousal higher.

It will also prevent her from coming, so it is for the best that she doesn't have too much.

There is no pain on her pretty face, only open-mouthed lust.

I slow my thrusts further, letting the hook penetrate deeper. Allowing it to open her.

Her groans turn guttural, face flushed, eyes wild. I lean in to kiss her again. Keeping her on the cusp—giving her enough to take the edge from the pain. Too much and she won't come. And I want her to fucking come all over my cock.

With each deep penetration, I feel the sensitive tip of my cock burrowing inside her womb. My sucker is inflamed to the point of madness, grasping at her swollen nubbin with each in stroke. Fuck, she is so tight. Sweat bathes my body, and her cries turn sharp.

"Just a little more, my sweet little human. Open for me like a good pet. Let your master in."

She is close to her limit.

I am close to my fucking limit.

But I need to get all the way fucking in.

HARPER

It helps when he kisses me, but he is not kissing me anymore. Deep inside, my pussy aches so bad, but my clit feels like he's sucking on it with every thrust, and it smothers the deepest pain. I don't understand what is happening to me. Through his dark sensuality, I've been broken down until I'm nothing but a whimpering bundle of need.

I'm hanging on the edge of a great cliff, and when I finally fall, I know I will discover the meaning of my life.

I can't endure more. Only I must, for he is not going to stop.

Tightening his hold on my waist, he slams deep. I feel something snap inside.

I'm broken; he has finally broken me.

Only there is no more pain. My clit is being sucked… by something, and I'm spinning so fast and hard that I need to cling to Quinn. My pussy convulses, and pleasure sweeps my whole body up. A wave of fire passing over my skin like a thousand pinpricks.

I'm hot.

Then I'm cold.

Then I'm coming all over again.

I make sounds like an animal as I hump furiously against the beastly male who has broken me on his huge alien cock.

"Good pet," he croons. "Milk your master of his seed."

His hands skim over me now. We are stuck together. I feel like I have been plugged so deeply by him that our bodies are one.

Shivers wrack my body, my teeth begin to chatter, and still the sucking thing works my clit, which in turn makes my pussy squeeze and gush around his thick alien cock.

"Good pet," he says, pressing kisses all over my cheeks and throat.

I cling to him. I'm so cold.

"Good pet," he says softly.

Then he pulls out, and I come all over again.

QUINN

I fear I have damaged the tiny human so briefly entrusted into my care. But to my surprise, she clings when I try to set her aside and check her. She is having none of it and weeps piteously against my chest. Laying on my back, I cradle her smaller body against mine. The emotions that assault me are complex, and I don't have a clue what any of them fucking mean.

It has been a long time since I sensed emotions... since I left the decimation of my home-world, to be exact. There are few beings I can read in this way, but the tiny human who has invaded my dreams is proving to be the first in many years.

And the emotions that are rolling from Harper are unmistakably the ones of fear. I want to protect her because I believe she is still in danger, although I don't know what from. Perhaps she fears the human male will return for her again.

I hold her tighter. Her anxiety sets my blood pounding. It is all I can do to keep my claws from springing and my horns from shifting to attack position.

"I want to be with you," she says between sobs. "Please don't leave me. I want to stay with you."

"I will not leave you," I say. "I promise. You are mine now. My little human pet and I will cherish and protect you for all our lives."

CHAPTER
TWELVE

HARPER

As I open my eyes to find dawn light leaking around the edges of my ill-fitted bedroom curtain, I'm assaulted by a sense of grief.

"No!"

I am home in my cruddy apartment with the peeling paint, broken extractor fan, and extra cold linoleum floors.

"No!" I sob the broken tears of someone who has had a hope and a dream snatched away. I wanted Quinn so badly. Wanted him with every fiber of my being. Then he was mine briefly, and now he has gone.

I don't even care that he wants to make me into some weird slave pet. I don't even care that he has a weird dick that did unnatural things to my pussy.

Beside me, lost in the covers, I hear the buzzing of my cell phone. I ignore it. Finally, I'm ready to admit that I need the kind of help that requires a person with qualifications. These hallucinations have got to stop.

After all Ned has put me through, it's a fictional character in a book that is the final straw to me seeking therapy.

Then I try to move. *Try.* What the fuck has happened to my body?

I still, heart thudding wildly and feeling faint. My throat stings a little, but it is nothing compared to the intimate place between my legs. It aches, an unnatural kind of ache from abused muscles that have been stretched around a huge alien... I'm not going there.

I'm hyperventilating. It's probably for the best that I'm still lying down.

I need to see. I need to know that I'm not losing my mind.

Heaving myself out of bed, I notice the tattered remnants of my clothing on the floor. Swallowing hard, I pad through to my tiny bathroom. With the light on, I examine my throat in the mirror. There, right there, I can see a row of half-moons where claws glanced the skin. As I hold my shaking finger up toward the marks, I can see they are not mine.

The feeling between my legs is assuredly not normal either. And deeper inside, it aches in a strange way, the place where he buried his hook.

As I stand hands braced to the sides of the small sink, I know what happened was real. Maybe this makes me officially crazy.

I need to find a way to Quinn.

Outside the bathroom, I can hear my cell buzzing incessantly.

I pad over and lift it up, squinting at the message.

It's pictures—lots and lots of pictures of Ned's pickup truck.

It's a message from Tammy.

What the fuck has happened to Ned's pickup! I heard through the grapevine he still owes some guy for it, and he's not been making the payments. Word is Ned has fled ahead of a smackdown from the guy he owes money to. He's not coming back, babe! You can come back home!

I snort out a laugh and shake my head.

Home? What is home anymore?

I don't fucking know, but it's not the town where I grew up and once lived with Ned. It's not here either, nor is it in another state.

On a frigid planet, somewhere far from here, is a stern alien with lethal claws who made a promise to me.

"I'm holding you to that promise, Quinn," I say. "The ball is in your court now."

QUINN

I wake up with a roar, for I am in bed and alone.

Again.

"Fuck!"

Once more, her scent lingers on my skin, but the pleasure is overwritten by the memory of her fear and of her sobbed begging to be with me.

I have fully claimed her. I have hooked her and latched my sucker to her nubbin.

I have planted my fucking seed for the first time in my life.

Rising, I throw on enough clothes that Haden will not castrate me in the presence of his mate and take off at a run. They are in Haden's office, along with Layton. Thank fuck no one else is here. Without a word, I lock the door and march over to where they stand examining the latest mining reports.

"Where are your fucking clothes?!" Haden demands, shoving his mate behind his back like I'm about to attack or molest her.

Layton clasps his long green fingers before him and radiates patience.

I look down at myself. I am wearing pants and boots. "I am decent," I say, frowning.

"What happened with the wormhole?" Layton asks. "I did warn you it was not an exact science."

"Yes, what happened?" Avery demands. Ignoring her mate's attempts to push her back behind him, she wriggles to the front.

"I went there," I say. "To her world. Where she was being attacked by her former mate."

"Oh my god!" Avery says. "Is she okay?"

"She was safe, last I saw. Her former mate—"

"Oh my god! Tell me you didn't kill him!" Avery says.

"Of course he killed him," Haden says, smirking. "Eliminate the competition. It is an accepted and reasonable approach."

"That is not a reasonable approach!" Avery says.

Haden encloses his big hand around the front of her throat and pulls her flush to his body. She squeaks and goes very still. He hasn't threatened to punish her again, but I believe it is what we are all thinking.

"I went to her world. I mated with her. But then I woke up here, and she was gone."

"Maybe she wants a less savage option?" Avery says, giving me a disparaging, up-down look that has my claws threatening to spring.

She gets a spank on her bottom for that and more cursing follows. The small human has the filthiest mouth.

"Harper doesn't want another option," I say. "She was afraid of the human male. She was frightened. She begged me to keep her. I made her a fucking promise that I would make her my pet. Now I have fucking failed, and she is gone."

"Fuck," Avery says, and she does not appear angry or disparaging anymore.

"Harper Reed does not have any context in this world," Layton says. The Lamandas male had been so silent, I had forgotten he was there. He turns toward Avery. "Might I venture to suggest she be given some context? The way you did when Haden brought you into this world."

"Avery is not fucking writing again," Haden says.

"I'm not leaving Harper there if she is frightened," Avery says, eyes narrowing in a way that suggests no level of threat or punishment will deter her. For the first time since I met the small, feisty human, I am unequivocally on her side.

"Although I'm not convinced about her choice," she adds, sending a withering look my way.

"Fine," Haden says. "How are we going to do this?"

"I don't think it matters how," Avery says. "I just need to write."

Layton takes his leave. There has been a breach in sector seventy-three, and he needs to manage the situation.

Which leaves me with Avery and Haden.

Haden sets up a computer for Avery to work on then puts her on his lap. I'm not allowed to look at what she is typing, which makes me fucking nervous. But I'm desperate. And every moment Harper is trapped on Earth is a moment too long.

"Tell us everything you know about her," Avery says.

So, I do, everything from a detailed description of how Harper looks to the intricacies of the recurring dream. Avery asks me some questions that make Haden growl. And some that make the fucker chuckle.

I pace. Avery writes. I pace some more.

Finally, she sits back and announces that she is done.

"Done?" I ask, expecting some magical event to whisk Harper to me or me to her. "What happens now?"

Avery's smile is all too knowing. "Now we wait and see."

"For what? What are we waiting for?" I want to rip my fucking horns from their sockets, I'm so frustrated.

The communicator bleeps. Avery dives to open the channel before Haden can intervene. He gives her a stern look. She returns an impish grin.

"Sir, we have an unexpected situation in the space dock that needs immediate attention," Layton says. "A freighter has an unexplained life-form aboard and are concerned a Narwan has entered the vessel. I was going to send Kane, but—"

"You are not fucking sending Kane!" I say already charging for the door.

"Put some clothes on, or you will fucking freeze!" Haden calls after me.

I do not put more clothes on. I head for the space dock at double time, open the airlock, and traverse the exposed space without a second thought.

HARPER

I spend the day in bed, listless to life. I feel sick inside my stomach and emotionally numb. I worry that I am going crazy, and I worry that I'm not. The slight sting at my throat and the ache inside my pussy are strange, and yet comforting reminders of what transpired.

Minutes drift into hours. I watch the glow increase behind the ill-fitting curtains, and I watch it fade again.

Forcing myself to get up, I make some toast and a cup of tea. Taking it back to bed, I munch without enthusiasm.

Tomorrow, I promise myself, I will get up and get on with my life. Ned has gone, fled according to Tammy, but I can't shake off the sick feeling that he might come back.

I don't sleep. I can't no matter how tired I get.

Then as I see the gray of dawn peeking around the edges of the curtains, I finally fall asleep.

I'm here, once again on the spacecraft. Only it's not like the previous times. Today, the metallic mesh flooring feels cold under my naked feet, and a weird chemical smell permeates the air. I reach out, touching the tall plastic crate beside me tentatively like I'm expecting it to disappear. Cool and smooth under my fingers, I stare at it in wonder.

I'm in my nightdress still. It's pink with a picture of a sleepy bear holding a book, and a caption, *I love bears, bedtime, and books.* I've had it for years. It's close to threadbare in places, but it's my favorite and I wear it all the time.

Coming from the distance is the sound of heavy footfall, *rapid,* heavy footfall. My heart rate jacks as I turn toward the entrance. I suck a deep breath in, bracing for whatever is about to come to pass. I don't hide. I'm rooted to the spot and confident my legs will give out if I try to take a single step.

The footsteps slow suddenly and then stop.

Is he there? Is it someone else? Why hasn't he come inside?

"Quinn?"

There is a closed door between us. Maybe he can't hear?

With a whoosh, the door springs open, and Quinn is standing there. He's wearing the bottom half of his black, futuristic armor and boots, leaving his upper body exposed. Frigid air wafts in through the open door and a little steam rises from his insanely built purple, dappled skin. In the amber lighting, he appears like a statue of an ancient Greek, half-animal god. His face has a compelling quality to it that has become hauntingly familiar to me. Dark hair too thick to be human, curving horns, a thick muscular neck leading down to great slabs of muscle that make up his arms, shoulders, chest, and abs.

I think he might be the most beautiful, primal being I have ever met.

"You made me a promise," I say softly. "Is this you keeping your promise?"

He steps forward, slow steps that bring him all the way up to me, until he's so close I'm forced to crane my neck to look up at him. Heat radiates from his body, and I shiver, reminding me of the cold flooring under my feet and the arctic air seeping into the room.

"Tiny, frail human," he says, voice a deep rumble that I feel vibrate through my chest. "You will not escape me again." Then his lips tug up showing way too many teeth

"I'm not hiding today," I say, feeling a sliver of hope unfurl inside my chest. If this is me sinking into a coma in the real world, then I pray no one wakes me up. "Today, I don't want to escape."

Smirking that slightly too wide, too many teeth smile, he clasps me around the waist and picks me up. I cling, curling my arms and legs around him, squeezing my body into his as tightly as I possibly can. Nose to the side of his throat, my breath turns stuttered and great heaving sobs bubble up. His arms are gentle as he cradles me to him, but I don't want gentle.

"You are not holding me tight enough," I say. "I think you might need to be all the way inside me so that I can't possibly escape."

He rumbles something between a groan and a growl. It vibrates through my body, and I feel my arousal rise.

"You are freezing, little stowaway, soon to be pet," he says. Turning, he strides out with me still clinging within his arms. As we exit the ship, I feel a great gust of icy wind.

"It is a short distance, and you will be warm," he rumbles.

He runs, jiggling me about in his arms. But it's soon over and we enter the great black fortress of Xars.

Inside he comes to an abrupt stop. I glance over my shoulder to see another hulking alien and a tiny earth woman.

"Oh!" I say inadequately. I did not remember any earth

women being on Xars in the book. "Are you trapped inside the book, too?"

Her lips open in a wide smile, and she chuckles. "Kind of. Actually, I wrote the book. Avery Sinclair, pleased to meet you, Harper. I thought Quinn was going to decimate the fortress if we didn't successfully bring you here."

"Avery Sinclair? Like the missing writer, Avery Sinclair?" I say, gaping.

She nods. "The very same. Only, I'm not missing. I'm exactly where I want to be. Now hopefully, so are you." Her face turns earnest. "You do want to be here, don't you?"

"Yes," I say, feeling Quinn's fingers tighten oh so slightly like he's worried I might be snatched away. "I want to be here very much."

EPILOGUE

HARPER

"That's good, pet," Quinn says, stroking his fingers through my hair. I'm on my knees, doing my best to suck his giant, alien cock. Not much fits in—the tentacle hook things at the end still freak me out—but they stay flush to the tip unless he's trying to breed me.

And yeah, that job is already done as my expanding waistline will attest.

His other hand is wrapped around the leash to my collar, and he tugs it every now and then to remind me that it's there.

I love that it's there.

I get hot thinking about it being there, and extra hot whenever Quinn draws my attention to it.

Which is often now that I consider it. My pregnancy hormones make me pretty needy.

Quinn also makes me needy. He doesn't even have to touch me, just walking into the room is enough to make my chest flutter and my pussy quiver.

I remember Avery checking when I first arrived that this was what I wanted.

I'm here because I want to be.

I'm here because I wished it.

I'm here because a mysterious missing writer, now a dear friend, wrote it in a book.

I'm here because I love the strange, compelling alien warrior who stormed into my life.

I'm here because this crazy is the perfect kind of right.

Thank you for reading Ravaged. I hope you enjoyed the book!

What's next in the series? Dive into book three, Avenged!

For free short stories, please check out BOOKS | FREE READS on my website www.AuthorLVLane.com

ALSO BY L.V. LANE

THE CONTROLLERS

COVETED PREY

VERITY ARDEN

Enjoyed L.V.'s books? You might also enjoy her contemporary pen name, Verity Arden!

In His Debt

Make Her Purr

Good With His Hands

Rough Around The Edges

ABOUT THE AUTHOR

In a secret garden hidden behind a wall of shrubs and trees, you'll find L.V. Lane's writing den, where she crafts adventures in fantastical worlds.

Best known for spicy adventures...Magical and mythical creatures, wolf shifters, and alphas of every flavor who give sweet and feisty omegas and heroines a guaranteed HEA, she also writes the occasional character-driven hard sci-fi full of political intrigue and action.

Subscribe to my mailing list at my website for the latest news: www.AuthorLVLane.com

- facebook.com/LVLaneAuthor
- x.com/AuthorLVLane
- instagram.com/authorlvlane
- amazon.com/author/lvlane
- bookbub.com/profile/l-v-lane
- goodreads.com/LVLane
- pinterest.com/authorlvlane
- tiktok.com/@covetedprey
- youtube.com/@authorLVLANE